Oliver Twist

by **Charles Dickens**
adapted by **Les Martin**
illustrated by **Jean Zallinger**

A STEPPING STONE BOOK™
Random House 🏠 New York

Text copyright © 1990 by Random House, Inc. Illustrations copyright © 1990 by Jean Zallinger. Cover illustration copyright © 1994 by José Miralles. All rights reserved under International and Pan-American Copyright Conventions. Published in the United States by Random House Children's Books, a division of Random House, Inc., New York, and simultaneously in Canada by Random House of Canada Limited, Toronto. Originally published by Random House, Inc., in 1990.

www.steppingstonesbooks.com
www.randomhouse.com/kids

Library of Congress Cataloging-in-Publication Data
Martin, Les, 1934–
Oliver Twist / by Charles Dickens ; adapted by Les Martin ; illustrated by Jean Zallinger.
   p. cm. — (A stepping stone book classic)
SUMMARY: A simple retelling of the adventures of the orphan boy who is forced to practice thievery and live a life of crime in nineteenth-century London.
ISBN 0-679-80391-2 (trade) — ISBN 0-679-90391-7 (lib. bdg.)
[1. Orphans—Fiction. 2. Robbers and outlaws—Fiction. 3. London (England)—Fiction.
4. Great Britain—History—19th century—Fiction.] I. Zallinger, Jean, ill. II. Charles Dickens, 1812–1870. Oliver Twist. III. Title. IV. Series.
PZ7.D55Ol 2006 [Fic]—dc22 2004019681

Printed in the United States of America 30 29 28 27 26 25 24 23

RANDOM HOUSE and colophon are registered trademarks and A STEPPING STONE BOOK and colophon are trademarks of Random House, Inc.

~ Oliver Twist ~

Chapter 1

"Please, sir, I want some more," the little boy said. He held out his food bowl. And his life was changed for-ever.

The boy's name was Oliver Twist. He did not get that name from his father. Nobody knew who his father was.

Nor from his mother. Nobody knew her name either. She had been found on the streets, sick and starving. A kind stranger brought her to a public workhouse. She gave birth to the boy. And died there soon after.

Mr. Bumble gave Oliver his name. Mr. Bumble ran the nearby orphans' home where Oliver was sent. Mr. Bumble was happy to take care of Oliver and all the other orphans. He had good reason to be.

The state paid to clothe and feed each child. Mr. Bumble got the money. And the orphans got rags on their backs and slop in their bellies.

No wonder Mr. Bumble was angry at Oliver. The very thought of a child asking for more to eat! Mr. Bumble saw his money being eaten up. Children's appetites were too big. Much too big for creatures so small.

So Oliver did not get any more greasy soup that night. He did not really expect to. He had asked for

more only because of the other starving orphans. They decided one of them had to speak up for all of them. They drew straws. Oliver lost.

Now it was Oliver alone who had to pay for this terrible crime.

"The boy will be hung someday," Mr. Bumble said sourly. But Mr. Bumble did not want to wait that long. He wanted Oliver out of the orphans' home quickly. Before others followed Oliver's evil ways.

First he locked Oliver away in a dark room. Then he went to Mr. Sowerberry, the local undertaker. He asked Mr. Sowerberry to take Oliver on as a helper.

Both gentlemen were pleased. Mr. Bumble would win praise. He had taken this ten-year-old burden off public welfare. And Mr. Sowerberry had the best kind of helper. A boy he could tell to do anything. And pay nothing.

As for Oliver, the boy had to be grateful. He would learn a good trade. People would need undertakers as long as they kept on dying.

But again Oliver proved to be ungrateful.

First he dared steal scraps from Mrs. Sowerberry's dear dog. Just because Oliver was close to starving.

Then Oliver did even worse. He punched Mr. Sowerberry's other helper, Noah Claypole. Right on Noah's large red nose. Noah was older than Oliver. Bigger and stronger. And thus worth more to Mr. Sowerberry.

And why did Oliver attack such a fine fellow? Only because Noah was clever enough to make a joke. But

Oliver did not find the joke funny. It was a joke about Oliver's mother. Oliver never knew his mother yet insisted on loving her.

Noah's nose was redder than ever when he went to the Sowerberrys. He told them about Oliver's brutal attack. They all agreed: next, Oliver would murder them in their beds.

Mr. Bumble was called. Mr. Bumble came. Mr. Bumble said the Sowerberrys had made a bad mistake. They had fed Oliver meat. Meat made children dangerous.

"Keep him a few days without food," Mr. Bumble advised. "Then feed him as I did. I promise you, that will teach him to be good."

Whether or not Mr. Bumble was right, no one would ever know. Oliver decided not to wait to find out.

That night Oliver made a bundle of all his spare clothes. A coarse shirt and two pairs of stockings. He put a stale crust of bread in his pocket. And a single penny given him as a tip at a funeral.

He crept out of the house into the cold night. Then he started walking on the highway. The highway to the great city of London.

Surely Mr. Bumble and Mr. Sowerberry would never find him there. Not among so many people. London was such a big city. Surely there would be a place for Oliver.

Indeed there was. But Oliver did not dream what kind of place it would be.

Chapter 2

London was sixty-five miles away. It was an easy trip by coach and horses. But not for a cold and hungry boy on foot.

It took Oliver six days. Six days of fearing he might be caught. Six days of trying to nap in fields. Six days of begging for water. Six days of farmers' dogs chasing him. Six days of doors slamming in his face.

Only bread bought with his one penny kept Oliver going. That, and food from a few kind souls along the way.

By the seventh day Oliver still had not reached London. He was in a village a mile from the city. Too tired to go farther, he sat huddled in a doorway. But it gave no shelter. The bitter cold cut into him like a knife.

Then he found what he wanted most in all the world. A friend.

Or rather, the friend found him.

This friend was the strangest boy Oliver had ever seen. He was no more than twelve, and small for his age. Yet he wore a man's coat. That coat reached almost to his heels. A man's hat sat on his head. That hat seemed ready to fall over his not-very-clean ears.

The boy found Oliver interesting-looking too. He glanced at Oliver

while walking past him. Then he
stopped. He came back and looked at
Oliver more closely.

"Hello. What's the problem?" he
asked.

"I am very hungry and tired," said

Oliver. "I have been walking these seven days."

"Seven days?" said the boy. "On the run from the beak, eh?"

"The beak?" asked Oliver.

"The law," explained the boy. "You been in the mill?"

"The mill?" asked Oliver.

"Jail," explained the boy. He grinned. "You're a green one. You got to learn the ropes. And I'm the one to teach you."

"I'd like it if you would," said Oliver.

"But first things first," the boy said. "Bet you wouldn't mind some eats, would you?"

"I . . . I wouldn't," Oliver admitted.

"Come on, then," said the boy. He led Oliver to a nearby eating place. There he ordered ham, cheese, bread, and something to drink. He paid the bill with a silver coin.

"Plenty more where that come from," he told Oliver. "Now tell me, what's your name?"

"Oliver, sir. Oliver Twist."

"I'm Jack Dawkins," the boy said. "But them that knows me calls me the Artful Dodger. Dodger, for short."

"Pleased to meet you, Mr. Dodger," Oliver said.

"You should be," said the Dodger. "You're going to London, right?"

"I am," said Oliver.

"And you don't got nowhere to stay," the Dodger said.

"I don't," agreed Oliver.

"No job, either," the Dodger added.

"No job," said Oliver.

"Just so happens I know a gentleman," the Dodger said. "A kind gentleman who loves to help out boys like you. And I am going to do you a great favor. I am taking you to that very same gentleman."

The Dodger got to his feet. He burped and patted his stomach.

"Look sharp now, Oliver," said the Dodger. "We're off to London town."

Chapter 3

Oliver had thought London was a city of beautiful houses and wide avenues. But the Dodger led him through narrow dirt streets lined with filthy buildings.

"This is London?" Oliver asked.

"Part of it," the Dodger said. "Welcome to Saffron Hill."

It was night. The shutters of the shops were closed. But drinking places were open everywhere. People who had had too much to drink lay outside them. Or maybe they had no-where but the streets to sleep.

"Makes you grateful for a good roof," said the Dodger. He stopped at the most run-down building on the run-down block. He banged on the door.

A voice shouted down, "Who's there?"

"*Me,*" the Dodger shouted back.

"Who's with you?" the voice asked.

"A new one," the Dodger replied.

"Come on up," the voice said.

"Got to give them warning," the Dodger told Oliver. "They don't trust strangers. Lot of nasty fellows around here."

The Dodger opened the peeling door. Oliver followed him up a shaky stairway. They went down a dark hallway to another door. A steel door.

The Dodger opened it.

"Oliver, meet the kind gentleman I told you about," the Dodger said.

The kind gentleman was standing by a fireplace. He was toasting sausages on a long fork. He turned. His smile showed yellow teeth above a matted red beard.

"Just cooking supper for my lads," he said. "You're welcome to join in, my dear boy."

There were four boys in the dark, dirty room. None was older than the Dodger.

Oliver already could see how kind the gentleman was. It had to cost him a pretty penny to care for these boys. Clearly he spent no money on himself. He wore a stained bathrobe and torn slippers.

"Oliver, meet Fagin," the Dodger said. "Fagin, this is Oliver Twist."

Fagin made a low bow. "Charmed to meet you, my dear," he said. He wrapped a sausage in a piece of black bread, then gave it to Oliver.

"Thank you, sir," said Oliver.

"A polite boy, a grateful boy," said Fagin. He turned to the others. "You all can take a lesson from him." Then he said to Oliver, "And you can learn a lot from them."

Supper was very greasy but very good.

"Before bed, we play a game," Fagin told Oliver after supper. "Watch a while. Then you can join in."

Fagin dressed himself in a fancy suit. In the pockets he put wallets, watches, and silk handkerchiefs. Then he started walking in a circle. He looked up at the ceiling and hummed to himself.

One by one the boys crept up behind him. The first slipped his hand into Fagin's pocket. He took out a watch. The next got a wallet. The third reached for a handkerchief. And got his hand slapped by Fagin.

"Clumsy, clumsy," Fagin said. "Won't do at all. Try harder."

Fagin began walking again. This time the boy did better. And won a fond pinch on his cheek.

"Very, very good," Fagin said. "You'll make your fortune yet."

When it was the Dodger's turn, he managed to grab a wallet *and* a watch *and* a handkerchief.

"You're a clever one," said Fagin. "Always said it, always will."

At last Oliver was allowed to share

the fun. Fagin let a handkerchief hang halfway out of his pocket. "See if you can take it without me feeling it."

Oliver crept up. Holding his breath, he slid the handkerchief out lightly.

Fagin clapped his hand to his empty pocket. "You got it! Wonderful. Here's a prize for you." He gave Oliver a coin.

"Keep on this way," said Fagin. "Someday you'll be a great man."

Oliver wondered how. Could playing this game *really* make him a great man? But he was sure the kind gentleman knew more than a boy.

"Bedtime, my dears," Fagin declared. "Tomorrow's a working day."

"Please, sir, what do they work at?" Oliver asked.

"Oh, they fix watches," said Fagin, holding up one. "And mend wallets.

Handkerchiefs, too. Of course, young boys make mistakes. These handkerchiefs, for instance. Charley Bates over there sewed on the wrong initials. Tomorrow, Oliver, perhaps you can help take them off."

"Oh yes, sir," said Oliver. "I do want to earn my keep." Then Oliver turned to the Dodger. "Thank you so much for bringing me here."

"I thank you too, Dodger," Fagin said. He rubbed his hands together. "You've brought us a real treasure."

Chapter 4

During the next few days, Oliver saw how much Fagin cared about his boys. Fagin wanted to bring them up right.

When they came back with watches, wallets, and handkerchiefs, Fagin patted their heads. And gave them extra sausage. But sometimes they came back empty-handed. Then Fagin got angry at them. He sent them to bed without supper.

"Hurts me more than you," he said. "But you must learn not to be lazy."

Oliver saw more of Fagin's kindness when two visitors arrived.

One was a tall man with a bad temper and big muscles. His name was Bill Sikes. The strong young woman with him was called Nancy. She was messy-looking but nice. Oliver liked her.

"Nancy grew up with me," Fagin said. "Now she devotes herself to helping Bill. Bill makes a fine living as, er, a salesman. And Nancy is all set to be his wife someday."

"Yeah, someday," Nancy said.

"Enough gab," Bill said. "How much for this?" He took silverware and silver candlesticks from his sack.

Fagin dropped a gold piece on the table. Bill's fist made the coin jump. Slowly Fagin let a few copper coins clink down.

"My limit," Fagin said.

Bill growled. Then he scooped up the money and left with Nancy.

"Lovely couple," Fagin said. "Wish I could help them more. But you boys are such a burden for a poor man."

"I know," said Oliver. "I'd like to do my full share. Please, sir, can I go out to work like the others?"

"A fine boy, a willing boy," said Fagin. He smiled at Oliver fondly.

When the Dodger heard the news, he said, "Knew you had the right stuff, Oliver. Come with me and Charley. We'll start you off right."

Oliver followed them through the streets to a nicer part of London. Well-dressed men and women strolled on clean sidewalks. The sun was bright. The air was sweet.

The Dodger stopped suddenly. He pointed to a bookstall across the street.

"See that old man with the white hair?" he asked quietly.

"Yes," said Oliver.

"Perfect!" said Charley Bates.

The man was reading a book with great interest. The Dodger and Charley nodded to each other.

Oliver saw the Dodger slink up to the gentleman. The Dodger's hand dipped into the gentleman's pocket. It pulled out a handkerchief.

For the first time Oliver knew what the "work" of Fagin's boys really was!

The bookstall owner shouted, "Stop, thief!"

The Dodger and Charley raced around a corner. Oliver saw only one thing he could do. Run!

Oliver ran right into a good citizen. That good citizen stopped Oliver. With the first thing that came to hand. A fist.

Oliver saw stars. Then blackness.

Finally that blackness brightened. Oliver opened his eyes. Yet he was sure he was dreaming.

Either that, or he had died and gone to heaven.

Chapter 5

Oliver woke up in a soft feather bed. A white-haired gentleman stood nearby. The gentleman whom the Dodger had robbed. But he did not look angry. He looked very pleased.

The gentleman spoke to his gray-haired housekeeper. "Mrs. Bedwin, the boy is awake."

"The doctor said he would get better, Mr. Brownlow," Mrs. Bedwin said. Her voice was happy.

"Have I been sick?" Oliver asked.

"You remember nothing?" asked Mr. Brownlow.

"Only running," Oliver said.

"It's just as well," Mr. Brownlow said. "The memory would be painful. People saw you running. They thought you were a thief.

"You were sent before a judge," Mr. Brownlow continued. "The meanest judge in London. Judge Fang himself. He was ready to send you to prison."

Mr. Brownlow smiled. "But the bookseller came in the nick of time. He said it was another boy who stole my handkerchief. Fang had to let you go. He looked as angry as a dog robbed of a bone."

"A dog has more human kindness than *him*," Mrs. Bedwin declared. "He didn't care that you were skin and bones. And burning up with fever. Thank heaven Mr. Brownlow could bring you home to be cared for."

"How long have I been here?" Oliver asked.

"Ten days," said Mr. Brownlow.

"Have I been sleeping all that time?" asked Oliver.

"Sleeping—and almost worse," said Mr. Brownlow. "But you're better. And you will get better still."

"With good food inside you," said Mrs. Bedwin.

"And with good clothes to wear. Good books to read. A good school to go to," Mr. Brownlow said.

"But that costs money," said Oliver. "I have none. Just as I have no place to live. Or father or mother. Or even a real name. Just Oliver Twist."

"I have more than enough money,"

Mr. Brownlow said. "And I have more than enough room for you in this house. I live here alone."

"Alone?" said Oliver. "But what about *her*?" He pointed to a picture hanging on the wall. A picture of a beautiful young woman.

"That picture was given to me by an old friend," said Mr. Brownlow. A shadow crossed his face. "I never knew the woman."

"It's odd," said Oliver. "I feel as if *I* know her. I feel as if she's trying to speak to me. Yet I can't make out a word."

"You're still weak from fever," said Mrs. Bedwin. She put a cool hand on his forehead. Her kind eyes studied his face. "Strange. You look a bit like her."

Mr. Brownlow looked carefully at

him too. "And from another angle, you look like—" He shook his head. "It does not matter.

"It is a small world," said Mr. Brownlow. "We are all related in a way. It is enough that you are you. And I will be like a father to you."

Oliver spent the next weeks in a new world. A world of love and kindness. He began to forget Fagin's den of thieves.

Mr. Brownlow's good friend Mr. Grimwig did not forget.

"That boy came from the underworld," Grimwig said. "And he'll go back to it."

"Never," said Mr. Brownlow.

"Then why does he not say whom he lived with?" Grimwig demanded.

"He doesn't want to get that person in trouble," Mr. Brownlow said.

"That person housed and fed the boy."

"You believe that?" Grimwig said. "You must believe in Father Christmas, too. Why not test the boy?"

Just then Mrs. Bedwin brought in some books. Mr. Brownlow had bought them from the bookstall that morning. The same bookstall where the Dodger had stolen his handkerchief. Mr. Brownlow wanted to return two books and pay his monthly bill. But the boy who delivered them to Mrs. Bedwin had left.

"Here is a perfect test," said Grimwig. "Send Oliver to pay your bill and return the books. I bet he will not come back."

"And if you're wrong?" said Mr. Brownlow, smiling. He knew how tough his friend liked to talk. He also knew how soft Grimwig's heart really was.

"Why, I will eat my own head," Grimwig declared. Mr. Brownlow chuckled.

Oliver was very happy to be of use. Mr. Brownlow gave him the money and the books. Off he rushed to the bookstall. And the two men waited for him to return.

They waited and waited. Hours passed. Darkness came. And gloom fell on the two old friends. Sadly they wondered what had become of Oliver.

Chapter 6

Oliver was back at Fagin's. Thanks to Nancy. She had tracked Oliver from the courtroom to Mr. Brownlow's home. Day after day she waited for Oliver to go out by himself. Then she grabbed him.

"Did he give you any trouble?" Fagin asked.

"He tried to," Nancy said. "A crowd gathered. But I pretended to be his sister. I said he had run away from home. People believed me, not him."

"Good girl," Fagin said. "I trained you well."

"Yes, you trained me," Nancy said. "You trained me to lie and steal and worse. I was no older than him."

"And here's the reward I promised," said Fagin. He gave her a gold piece.

"Keep your other promise, too," Nancy said. She grabbed his wrist and squeezed it. "Don't harm the boy."

"Of course not, my dear," said Fagin. "You women. So tender when it comes to children."

"The last piece of tenderness left in me," said Nancy.

"What about your feelings for Bill Sikes?" said Fagin.

"That ain't tenderness. That's weakness," said Nancy with a shrug.

"Well, *my* weakness is for lads like

Oliver," said Fagin. He patted Oliver on the head. "In fact, I have a *special* weakness for Oliver."

"Why him?" asked Nancy.

"That's for me to know. And no one else to find out," said Fagin.

42

Nancy's eyes narrowed. "Does it have to do with that stranger? The one who came to see you last week? After his visit, you promised gold for finding the kid. Before, it was just silver."

Fagin's voice was hard. "Curiosity can kill more than a cat, Nancy." Then he softened his voice. "Forget that man. He had nothing to do with it. I just didn't want the brat to spill the beans. On us all."

Oliver saw his chance to speak up. "Sir, I never said a word. Please, let me go back to Mr. Brownlow. I'll keep quiet. I swear I will." Oliver swallowed hard. "I swear on my poor mother's grave."

"Very touching, my dear boy," Fagin said. "But you know too much. I will never let you go."

"Then let me send Mr. Brownlow the money he gave me," said Oliver. "Or else he will think I stole it."

This made Fagin laugh. "What a clever boy to think of that. I'm glad you know you are now a thief. In the eyes of Mr. Brownlow. In the eyes of the law. In the eyes of all the world."

Oliver had to bite his lip to keep from crying. Fagin was right. Oliver might escape again. But Mr. Brownlow would never take him back.

Fagin pinched Oliver's cheek. "Thank you for the money. And your nice new clothes. Still, you must earn your keep. Learn your trade."

Fagin smiled. "If you are a thief, you had better be a good one. But you're in luck. We have a fine teacher for you. The best. Bill Sikes himself."

"Did I hear my name?" a voice roared.

It was Bill Sikes. His big body filled the doorway. He stomped into the room. He glared at Fagin.

"I don't like to hear my name spoke. Can be dangerous," he snarled.

Bill had his big, flea-bitten white dog with him. The dog snarled too. Bill gave it a kick that sent it whimpering into a corner.

"Hear that, Oliver," Fagin said. "You don't want to say Bill Sikes's name to anybody."

Bill put his huge hands on Oliver's neck. "You do," he growled, "and I'll rip your head clean off."

"Go easy on him, Bill," Nancy begged. "He ain't done nothing to you."

"Stay out of this, Nancy. Or I'll beat the stuffing out of you," said Bill. He turned to Fagin. "This the kid you promised me?"

"The perfect one for the job," Fagin assured him. "Sent by heaven, you

might say." Fagin rubbed his hands together. "You owe me a little something for his help. As agreed."

"You'll get your cut *after* the job," said Bill.

His hand closed on Oliver's thin

shoulder. "Time to go to work. Our time. Nighttime."

"Your new life is starting, Oliver," Fagin said. "Get used to it. It's the only life you'll have. Until the day you die."

Chapter 7

"Here's a lesson for you," said Bill Sikes once they left. He pressed a gun against Oliver's head. "Obey me or else."

Then Bill dragged Oliver to a big house outside of London. The night was dark and damp. Bill opened a small high window.

"You're going in that window and straight ahead," said Bill. "Unlock the front door and let me in. If you get any ideas, remember this." He tapped his gun against the boy's head.

Oliver knew Bill was going to rob the house. Or worse. Bill lifted him up and lowered him through the window. He gave Oliver a lantern.

Oliver crept through the hall. He heard footsteps upstairs. And Bill Sikes hollering, "Come back! Back!" The lantern crashed.

The last thing Oliver remembered was the sound of a gun. And pain.

At last Oliver opened his eyes. He saw an angel. Or a young woman as beautiful as an angel.

"I'm Rose," she said. "And this is my aunt, Mrs. Maylie." Oliver saw an older woman with a sweet face. "And this is our friend, Dr. Losberne. He saved your life after our servant shot you."

"I don't think you'll be robbing people for quite a while," said the doctor.

"Please, sir," said Oliver. He was still pale and weak. But he could not bear being taken as a thief. He told his sad story.

Everyone who heard him knew he was telling the truth. "He is so young," said the doctor.

"Young enough for a better life," Rose said. "We must show him a better way."

And Rose and Mrs. Maylie knew a better way. Love and kindness. They nursed Oliver back to health in their country house.

There was good food to eat and milk to drink. Dr. Losberne brought Oliver all the books he could read.

There were days of play in the sunshine. And evenings when Rose played the piano.

Only one thing was worrying Oliver. He wanted Mr. Brownlow to know he was not a thief. He asked Dr. Losberne to find him.

But Mr. Brownlow and his housekeeper had moved. So had his friend Grimwig. No one knew how or why.

But that was the only cloud in Oliver's life. The only cloud, for months and months. Until one late summer evening.

The sun was setting. Oliver was in a room facing the garden. He was reading a long book and was getting drowsy. The printed words blurred. He began to half dream.

He saw Fagin again and the Dodger. Bill Sikes and Nancy. Mr.

Bumble and Mr. Sowerberry. The dream was getting worse and worse. He forced his eyes open.

Fagin's face was right outside the window! Another man was with Fagin. Oliver did not know that man. But he knew the look in the man's eyes. Burning hate.

Oliver screamed. The way one screams in a nightmare. Rose came running.

Fagin and the other man had vanished. Rose found Oliver alone. He was shivering in the warm summer air. Fear was on his face.

"What's wrong?" she asked. "You look as if you saw a ghost."

"I wish it was a ghost," Oliver said. "I wish my past was dead. But it is not. I know that now."

"I have never asked you more about your past," Rose said. "I wanted you to forget it. But now I must know what frightened you so."

"I saw Fagin here. The man who tried to make me a thief," said Oliver. "I do not know the man who was with him. Yet somehow I thought I knew his face."

Oliver sighed. "I know why Fagin was here. He came to get me back. Just like he did before, when I was at Mr. Brownlow's. Except that time he used someone else to help him."

"Who?" asked Rose.

"A girl. But more than a girl. I think Nancy is about your age," Oliver said.

Then it was Rose's turn to show fear.

"A young woman just knocked on the door," Rose said. "I let her in and asked her name. Her name is— Nancy."

Chapter 8

"Don't believe Nancy," Oliver begged Rose. "She'll tell you lies. Anything to take me back to Fagin."

"It's you I believe," Rose promised him. "We'll face her together. We'll make short work of her lies."

But Nancy had not come to tell lies. Her face was pale and frightened.

"Listen to what I say. I risk my life to say it," she said. "But better my life than the boy's. He has some hope of a better life. I have none."

"But you are still so young," Rose said. She was shocked by the sadness in Nancy's voice.

"Young in years," Nancy said. "But old in every other way. Too old to change. But enough about me. I must tell you about Oliver. While there is still time to save him."

"I'm listening," said Rose.

"Listen closely. As closely as I did at Fagin's," Nancy said. "I was there when a man came to see him. A young, well-dressed man."

Nancy paused. "I had seen him once before. When Oliver was gone the first time. This time I wanted to find out who the man was. What he wanted."

"Did you?" Rose asked.

"I did," Nancy said. "I pretended to be sound asleep in the corner. They thought I had had too much to drink.

So they talked freely. And what I heard made me come here."

"Please, what did you hear?" asked Oliver. Why would a well-dressed man visit Fagin? What could his visit have to do with Oliver?

"Fagin called him Mr. Monks," Nancy said. "He and Fagin come from different worlds. I could see that. But they're birds of a feather."

Nancy sighed. "Monks said it was his good luck to spot Oliver with the Dodger. It was that day at the book-stall. He guessed who Oliver was right away. And he could tell the Dodger was a thief. Then the police grabbed Oliver."

Nancy's voice was sad. "Monks paid the Dodger to lead him to Fagin. He wanted Fagin to turn the boy into a thief. Imagine that! A thief who would end his life in jail.

"But," continued Nancy, "that nice gentleman came along to spoil Monks's plan. So Monks paid Fagin to get Oliver back. Next Monks went to an orphans' home run by a Mr. Bumble. Monks wanted to make sure he was right about Oliver."

"He knew who I was?" Oliver asked eagerly. "Tell me, who am I?"

"Monks didn't say," said Nancy. "He just gave a nasty laugh. And called you his 'little brother.' "

"What did he mean?" Rose wondered.

"I have no idea, miss," said Nancy. "But he did say something strange. That *you'd* give the world to know who Oliver is."

"*Me?*" Rose said.

"That's right," said Nancy. "Monks

thought it a big joke that Oliver was with you. That it was your house where Bill left Oliver for dead."

"A joke?" Rose shuddered. "How terrible."

"Worse is to come," said Nancy.

"Worse?" said Oliver.

"Monks had bought a locket from Mr. Bumble," Nancy said. "That locket was the last hope of anyone saving Oliver. Monks dumped it in the river. Now Fagin could feel safe in doing

what he wanted with Oliver."

Nancy wiped away some tears and continued. "Monks stood by the offer he had made. He would pay Fagin for making Oliver a thief. Monks wanted the pleasure of seeing Oliver in jail. Or on the gallows."

"Fagin agreed?" said Rose. "I can't believe anyone is that evil."

"You don't know Fagin," Nancy said. "He'll do anything for money."

"Did you find out anything more about the locket?" Oliver asked.

"Nothing," Nancy said.

"Nothing?" said Oliver. His heart sank. He had felt so close to finding out who he was. Now he was back in the dark.

"But there is someone who may tell you more," Nancy said.

"Who?" asked Oliver.

"I do not know his name. And he does not know mine," said Nancy. "That was our agreement. But I can take you to him."

"Please do!" Oliver exclaimed.

"Yes, please!" Rose echoed.

Rose's aunt was napping upstairs. They left her a note saying they would be back soon. Then they found a cab. Nancy gave the driver an address. The man cracked his whip. His horse trotted smartly to a hotel in the heart of the city.

Nancy led them to a room on the third floor. She knocked on the door. It opened. And Oliver thought his heart would burst with joy.

"Mr. Brownlow!" he said.

Chapter 9

Oliver and Mr. Brownlow hugged each other. Then Oliver introduced Rose. First to Mr. Brownlow. Then to Grimwig, who was also there.

"Grimwig thought Oliver was a thief when he did not come back," Mr. Brownlow said.

Grimwig coughed. "I did not want to. But I am a lawyer. I go by evidence."

"I had different evidence," Mr. Brownlow said. "The evidence of my heart. The evidence of my eyes."

"Of course," Rose said. "Anyone can see Oliver is no thief."

"I saw even more than that," Mr. Brownlow said. "When I saw Oliver's face, I saw another face as well. The face of a man who was my dear friend years ago. And I saw another, too. The woman my friend loved. The woman whose picture he left with me."

"The picture of the beautiful lady in my room?" Oliver asked.

"The same," said Mr. Brownlow.

"I felt as if I somehow knew her," Oliver said. "Please, sir, what is her name?"

"My friend would not tell me," Mr. Brownlow said. "He wanted to protect her. You see, his family had pushed him to marry. He was very young. It was a mistake. When he and his wife parted, she went to Europe with their son. A terrible young man. A great disappointment to his father."

Mr. Brownlow sighed. "My friend stayed here and met the girl he loved. Love made him lie. He told her he was single and married her. But when she was expecting a baby, he had to stop living that lie. He went to Europe to end his first marriage.

"But first," continued Mr. Brownlow, "he made a will. It gave his first wife and their son half his fortune when he died. The rest would go to the woman he loved and their child.

"He left me the painting of his love before he sailed. He painted it himself. A surprise for her when he returned."

"What became of him?" asked Oliver.

"A month later I read in the paper that he had died," Mr. Brownlow said. "I wrote to his wife in Europe for more news. She did not answer. I tried to find out who the woman he loved was. But I failed."

"That is all you know?" asked Oliver. He could not hide his disappointment.

"That is all I knew then," Mr. Brownlow said. "I know more now. After you vanished, Oliver, I again searched for that missing woman. I sensed a bond between her and you. By finding her, I might find you."

"Did you? Find *her*, I mean?" Oliver asked eagerly.

"Yes, did you?" asked Rose. She seemed as interested as Oliver was.

"Yes. And no," said Mr. Brownlow. "I again tried to contact my friend's first wife. She had died. The only person left to ask was her son. But he had moved to the West Indies. I shut up my house in London and sailed there. Grimwig came with me. He wanted to find Oliver as much as I did."

Grimwig's ears grew pink. "I wanted evidence, that's all."

"Did you find it, Mr. Grimwig?" asked Oliver.

Mr. Brownlow shook his head. "No, he didn't. My friend's son was gone. His business had failed. He had come back here. We came back too and found him. But he would not talk about his father. He said he wanted to cut all ties with the past. He had even changed his name. Now he calls himself Monks."

"Monks!" Nancy said.

"Do you know him?" Mr. Brownlow demanded. "I know you do not want to betray the people you live among.

We agreed on that when you answered my poster. My poster asking about Oliver and offering a reward. But things have changed."

"They have," Nancy agreed. "That is why I went to Miss Maylie. That is why I brought her and Oliver to you."

Suddenly Nancy's eyes turned nervously to a clock. "Miss Maylie can tell you the rest," she said. "I have stayed away too long already. I will be missed."

"Before you go—" Mr. Brownlow said. He pulled out his wallet.

"No," Nancy said. "Once in my life, I want to do something *not* for money. Just once before I die."

Chapter 10

Nancy left. Grimwig went to the window. "I'll see where she is heading," he said.

"Do not spy on her," Mr. Brownlow said. "We cannot use her to go after her friends. We promised not to." He turned to Rose. "Please, tell me what you have learned."

Rose told him Nancy's story. Mr. Brownlow nodded.

"I know most of it already," he said. "You see, I hired a detective to follow

Monks. Monks led him to Fagin's door. Then to the orphans' home.

"So," said Mr. Brownlow, "I went and questioned that same Mr. Bumble. I paid him to give me answers. He told me about selling Monks the locket. The locket had belonged to a lovely young woman who had died. She had come to the workhouse. It was next door to the orphans' home. The young woman gave birth to a baby before she died."

"A baby?" said Oliver.

"A baby boy," said Mr. Brownlow.

"Did Mr. Bumble tell you that boy's name?" asked Oliver.

"He did. When I gave him still more money," Mr. Brownlow said. He put his hand on Oliver's shoulder. "I think you can guess that name. The name Bumble gave that boy."

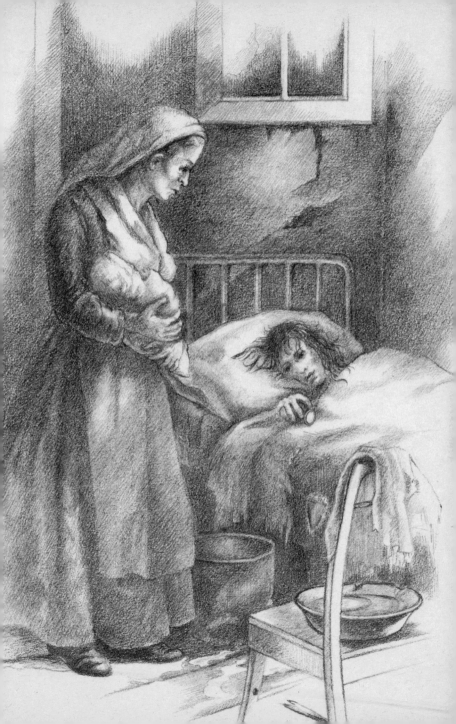

"My name," gasped Oliver. "The lovely young woman was my mother. The woman with the locket."

"Did Bumble tell you more about the locket he sold to Monks?" Rose asked. Her voice was excited.

"He did, for more money. I have never seen a man so greedy," said Mr. Brownlow.

He smiled. "Bumble will need every penny I gave him. I have reported what he did. Mr. Bumble no longer has a job. And will not soon find another."

"But what did he say about the locket?" Rose asked again.

"Only that it was gold. And had a single name on it," Mr. Brownlow said.

"What was that name?" asked Rose.

"Agnes," Mr. Brownlow answered.

Rose's face became pale. Her voice

shook. "And Monks's real name?"

"Edward Leeford," Mr. Brownlow answered. "Why do you ask?"

"My only sister was named Agnes," Rose said. "She had such a locket. And she married a man named Leeford."

"The man who was my friend," said Mr. Brownlow. "Monks's father."

"He took Agnes to live in another town," said Rose. "She wrote me she was going to have a child. Then I heard no more. I went to see her. She was gone. No one knew where. But now I know."

"Does that mean—" Oliver began to ask. He could not finish his question. His heart was beating too hard.

"It means my sister was your mother," Rose said. She gave Oliver a giant hug. "I am your aunt. And will be like a mother to you."

"Amazing," said Mr. Brownlow. He shook his head in wonder.

"But sir, you once told me it is a small world," Oliver said. "You said we are all related."

"I did not know how true that was," said Mr. Brownlow. He wiped tears from his eyes. Tears of joy.

"True indeed. Very true," Mr. Grimwig said. He wiped his eyes too. "Must have gotten a speck in them," he said. He used his handkerchief to polish his glasses. Then Mr. Grimwig cleared his throat. "This evidence is true enough to stand up in court. Monks will have to pay Oliver what he owes him. Half his father's fortune." He smiled at Oliver. "What will you do with your money? Buy toys? Sweets?"

"I'll give most of it to Nancy," Oliver

said. "She needs it more than I do. I have all of you. But she has only mean Bill Sikes and evil Fagin."

"She has another friend, too," Mr. Grimwig said. "I saw him when I looked out the window. His eyes lit up when he saw Nancy."

"What did he look like?" asked Oliver. Fear was in his voice.

Mr. Grimwig smiled. "Don't worry, Oliver. He was little more than a child. He looked as if he were going to a costume party. All dressed up in grown-up clothes."

"The Dodger," said Oliver.

"The Dodger?" said Mr. Brownlow.

"He's one of Fagin's boys," said Oliver. "The one who stole your handkerchief. Fagin had him follow Nancy. Now he'll tell Fagin that Nancy came here. Fagin won't like it. Bill will like it even less. We must save Nancy."

Oliver was already at the door.

"Surely we do not need to rush so," Mr. Grimwig said. "We'll go to the police. Let them take over."

"You don't know how fast the Dodger moves," Oliver said. "Or how quick-tempered Bill is. *Hurry!*"

Chapter 11

They rushed out of the hotel. Mr. Brownlow hailed a cab.

"Hurry," Mr. Brownlow told the driver. He gave him an extra gold piece.

The cab wove through the traffic. But it stopped when it reached the slums. The driver said, "This is as far as I go. The streets are too narrow here. Too dangerous."

Oliver, Mr. Brownlow, Grimwig, and Rose went on by foot.

"I'll go first," said Oliver. He led them through the twisting streets to where Nancy and Bill Sikes lived.

A crowd was in front of the building. And police, too.

"What happened, Officer?" Mr. Brownlow asked one of the police-men.

"A murder," he said.

Oliver's heart sank. His voice shook.

"Who was murdered, sir?"

"A girl. Nancy something," the policeman said. "Seems the killer was waiting for her. Beat her to death on the spot. Who knows why. These people are animals."

"Not animals. All too human," said Mr. Brownlow. "That poor girl. Have you caught the killer?"

"He got clean away," said the policeman. "It'll be a job to hunt him down. This place is a jungle."

"A reward for finding the killer!" Mr. Brownlow shouted to the crowd.

"And I'll add something to it!" Grimwig shouted.

"We'd do it for nothing," a man in the crowd said. "Nancy was a good sort. But it was Bill Sikes who done it. Bill is clever as a fox. Lord only knows where he's hiding out."

Just then a dog came running out of the building. A big white dog.

A policeman came running after it. "It got out of the girl's room," he said. "Must have belonged to her."

"Not to her. To Bill Sikes," said Oliver. "Quick! Follow it!"

The dog ran yelping through the streets. It knew where it was going. The crowd ran after it. The number of people kept growing. Everyone wanted to catch Nancy's killer.

The dog stopped at a building. It howled and clawed at the front door.

"Fagin's place," Oliver said.

"Break the door down!" shouted a man in the crowd.

"Get a battering ram!" shouted a woman.

Someone found a large beam of wood. Five strong men bashed it against the door. The door caved in.

The crowd started to pour through it. Then Oliver shouted, "Look! Up there! At Fagin's window!"

The people stopped in their tracks. They looked up at the high window. Bill Sikes stood on the ledge.

"Give yourself up!" a policeman called to him.

"You'll never catch me!" Bill shouted back. He leaped to the roof of the next building. An amazing jump for someone so big.

Bill ran over the rooftops, leaping from one to another. On the streets below, the crowd followed him.

He reached the last building before the river. But that did not stop him. He was carrying a coil of rope. He tied one end around a chimney. He made the other end into a loop.

He put the loop over his head.

Oliver heard a man in the crowd ask, "What the devil is he doing?"

"Can't you see?" another answered. "He'll put the loop around his waist. He'll lower himself down to the river. And he'll swim for it. That fox. He'll cheat the hangman yet."

But suddenly Bill froze. His eyes grew big. He screamed, "Nancy! What are you doing here? Take your eyes off me! Your eyes!"

Nobody could see what Bill was staring at. But everyone saw him take a step backward. Right off the roof.

He fell through empty air. Until his fall was stopped by the rope. The rope around his neck.

The crowd was quiet for a moment. They watched the dead man swinging on the rope.

Then someone said, "It was like he saw a ghost."

Another added, "I said he'd cheat the hangman. He did the job himself."

The crowd broke up. But the police were still on the job. And Oliver and his friends still had work to do.

They all headed for Fagin's place.

Chapter 12

The police pounded on Fagin's door. It was made of steel. Too hard to break open.

"Open in the name of the law!" a policeman shouted.

"You're wanted for hiding a killer!" shouted another. "You won't get away from us. Not this time."

They heard Fagin's voice from inside. "I'll never give myself up! Unless we make a deal."

"What kind of deal?" a policeman replied.

"I'll hand over a gang of thieves to you," said Fagin. "I'll give evidence against them. It's a good trade. You get five evil boys. You just have to let one poor, harmless old man go free."

"Forget it," the policeman called back. "You're coming with us."

"Nev—" Fagin started to shout. Then his voice was cut off. A moment later the door swung open.

Charley Bates stood there. Behind him the Dodger was sitting on Fagin's chest. The other boys held down Fagin's arms and legs.

"After all I've done for you," Fagin moaned.

"And what you wanted to do *to* us," the Dodger replied. He looked at the police. "Give us a break for helping nab Fagin. How about it?"

"Tell it to the judge," a policeman said. He pulled Fagin to his feet. And put handcuffs on him.

"Oliver!" Fagin cried. "Tell them I meant no harm, my dear. I was like a father to you. To all the boys."

Oliver looked right into Fagin's eyes. He said not a word.

"Why, you little—" screamed Fagin. He tried to leap at Oliver. But the policemen were holding him tightly.

"Time to get what's coming to you," the head policeman said. "Take them away, fellows."

Police surrounded Fagin and the boys. They left for jail.

Only Oliver and his friends remained. Plus one other person. A well-dressed young man. A young man in the corner. A young man who shrank from Mr. Brownlow's eyes.

"So this is where I find you, Edward Leeford," Mr. Brownlow said. "Or should I call you Monks?"

"I can explain everything," Monks said.

"We already know everything," Mr. Brownlow said.

"Except one thing," said Mr. Grimwig. "Where is the will?"

"What will?" asked Monks.

"Your father's will," said Mr. Grimwig. "The will that left half his fortune to your half-brother, Oliver."

"There is no such will," said Monks.

"There *is* one," Mr. Brownlow said. There was iron in his voice. "Your father told me of it. I will swear to that in court. *If* you make us take you there."

"I was afraid someone knew about it," Monks said in a broken voice. "But it said that if Oliver ever broke the law, he'd get nothing. Then I'd be safe."

"Talk, talk," Grimwig said impatiently. "Answer my question. Where is the will?"

"My mother destroyed it," Monks said. "Then she wrote to Oliver's mother, Agnes. She said that my father was already married. And wanted nothing more to do with Agnes."

"How hurt poor Agnes must have been," said Rose. "How ashamed. No wonder she ran away."

"Well, it seems you are a wealthy young man," Mr. Brownlow told Oliver. "You have half of Leeford's fortune."

"But that is all that is left," Monks protested. "I have had bad luck in business. And even worse luck gambling. I will be left without a penny."

"Then learn from Oliver," said Grimwig. "*He* did not have a penny.

And he has come far in the world."

"A fortune," said Oliver. "What will I do with it?"

"I will watch over it until you are grown up," said Mr. Brownlow. "Then you can do what you want with it."

"And I will take care of you while

you grow up," said Rose. She held him close. "I will be your second mother."

"It all seems too good to be true," said Oliver.

But it was true.

Then and in the years to come.

For Oliver and all who loved him.

Les Martin has adapted *The Time Machine* as well as *Oliver Twist* for the Stepping Stones series. He has visited many foreign countries, and his travels help him re-create the feel of whatever place he writes about. Mr. Martin lives in New York City.

Jean Zallinger has illustrated more than eighty children's books, most of them on natural history topics. She is a retired college professor who enjoys traveling, writing, and working with children. She and her husband, who is also an artist, live in North Haven, Connecticut.